The Night Before Christmas

By Clement C. Moore

Illustrated by Mircea Catusanu

A GOLDEN BOOK • NEW YORK

Golden Books Publishing Company, Inc., New York, New York 10106

© 2001 Golden Books Publishing Company, Inc. All rights reserved. Printed in the U.S.A. No part of this book may be reproduced or copied in any form without written permission from the copyright owner. GOLDEN BOOKS®, A GOLDEN BOOK®, A LITTLE GOLDEN BOOK®, G DESIGN®, and the distinctive spine are registered trademarks of Golden Books Publishing Company, Inc. Library of Congress Catalog Card Number: 00-102796   ISBN: 0-307-96003-X   First Edition 2001
10 9 8 7

'Twas the night before Christmas,
when all through the house,

Not a creature was stirring, not even a mouse.
The stockings were hung by the chimney with care,
In hopes that St. Nicholas soon would be there.

The children were nestled all snug in their beds,
While visions of sugarplums danced in their heads.

And Mamma in her kerchief, and I in my cap,
Had just settled down for a long winter's nap.
When out on the lawn there arose such a clatter,
I sprang from the bed to see what was the matter.

Away to the window I flew like a flash,
Tore open the shutters and threw up the sash.
The moon on the breast of the new-fallen snow,
Gave the luster of midday to objects below.

When, what to my wondering eyes should appear,
But a miniature sleigh and eight tiny reindeer.
With a little old driver, so lively and quick,
I knew in a moment it must be St. Nick.

As dry leaves that before the wild hurricane fly,
When they meet with an obstacle, mount to the sky,
So up to the housetop the coursers they flew,
With the sleigh full of toys, and St. Nicholas, too.

And then in a twinkling, I heard on the roof,
The prancing and pawing of each little hoof—

As I drew in my head, and was turning around,
Down the chimney St. Nicholas came with a bound.

He was dressed all in fur, from his head to his foot,
And his clothes were all tarnished with ashes and soot.
A bundle of toys he had flung on his back,
And he looked like a peddler just opening his pack.

His eyes, how they twinkled! His dimples, how merry!
His cheeks were like roses, his nose like a cherry!
His droll little mouth was drawn up like a bow,
And the beard on his chin was as white as the snow.

The stump of his pipe he held tight in his teeth,
And the smoke, it encircled his head like a wreath.
He had a broad face and a little round belly,
That shook when he laughed, like a bowl full of jelly.

He was chubby and plump, a right jolly old elf,
And I laughed when I saw him, in spite of myself.

A wink of his eye and a twist of his head,
Soon gave me to know I had nothing to dread.
He spoke not a word, but went straight to his work,
And filled all the stockings, then turned with a jerk.

And laying his finger aside of his nose,
And giving a nod, up the chimney he rose.

He sprang to his sleigh, to his team gave a whistle,
And away they all flew like the down of a thistle.
But I heard him exclaim, as he drove out of sight,

"Happy Christmas to all.
And to all a good night."